LICKING COUNTY LIBRARY
NEWARK, OHIO 43055-5054

NEW ORLEANS
HORNETS

by Paul D. Bowker

Published by ABDO Publishing Company, 8000 West 78th Street, Edina, Minnesota 55439. Copyright © 2012 by Abdo Consulting Group, Inc. International copyrights reserved in all countries. No part of this book may be reproduced in any form without written permission from the publisher. SportsZone™ is a trademark and logo of ABDO Publishing Company.

Printed in the United States of America,
North Mankato, Minnesota
062011
092011

 THIS BOOK CONTAINS AT LEAST 10% RECYCLED MATERIALS.

Editor: Dave McMahon
Copy Editor: Anna Comstock
Series design: Christa Schneider
Cover production: Craig Hinton
Interior production: Carol Castro

Photo Credits: Patrick Semansky/AP Images, cover, 6, 39, 43 (bottom); Chuck Burton/AP Images, 1, 12, 16, 42 (middle); Matt Slocum/AP Images, 4; Amy Sancetta/AP Images, 9; Marty Lederhandler/AP Images, 10, 42 (top); Bill Kostroun/AP Images, 15; Ron Frehm/AP Images, 19; Beth A. Keiser/AP Images, 21; Rick Havner/AP Images, 22, 42 (bottom); Ron Schwane/AP Images, 24; J.P. Moczulski/AP Images, 26; Bill Haber/AP Images, 29, 36, 43 (middle), 47; David J. Phillip/AP Images, 30, 43 (top); Andrew J. Cohoon/AP Images, 33; Sue Ogrocki/AP Images, 34; Mark J. Terrill/AP Images, 40; Chris Carlson/AP Images, 44

Library of Congress Cataloging-in-Publication Data
Bowker, Paul, 1954-
  New Orleans Hornets / by Paul D. Bowker.
      p. cm. -- (Inside the NBA)
  Includes index.
  ISBN 978-1-61783-167-6
  1. New Orleans Hornets (Basketball team)--History--Juvenile literature. I. Title.
  GV885.52.N375B69 2012
  796.323'64'0976335--dc23

                          2011021374

TABLE OF CONTENTS

CHAPTER 1

SOUTHWEST CHAMPS

Mascot Hugo the Hornet made his first appearance at the Charlotte Coliseum in North Carolina in 1988. After 20 years and three different homes, Hugo's National Basketball Association (NBA) team, the Hornets, had finally settled in New Orleans.

And on an April evening in 2008, the New Orleans Hornets gave fans in their new home in Louisiana a reason to celebrate.

A 32-point game by forward David West helped the Hornets to a 114–92 victory over the Los Angeles Clippers. The win came in front of a sellout crowd. And it gave the Hornets their first NBA divisional championship. More than 17,000 fans celebrated a memorable night for a team that had survived a hurricane, a move from Charlotte, and plenty of doubters.

"A lot of people had us not even getting in the playoffs," Hornets center Tyson Chandler said.

New Orleans point guard Chris Paul led the Hornets to their first Southwest Division title in 2008.

Hornets head coach Byron Scott, *right*, celebrates with Chris Paul, *middle*, and David West, *left*, during a game in 2010.

"It's a big step for us," West said. "We just talked about wanting to improve and being one of the elite teams."

Just a few years earlier, winning an NBA Southwest Division championship seemed out of reach for New Orleans.

In 2004–05, the Hornets won just 18 games. Then Hurricane Katrina devastated the city of New Orleans in 2005.

Katrina was one of the worst hurricanes in US history, and it tore apart New Orleans. It caused more than an estimated $125 billion in economic and housing losses. Thousands of residents lost their homes and jobs. Schools were closed. The Hornets had to leave New Orleans for a period of time after the disaster. They had to play most of their home games more than 700 miles (1,126 km) away in Oklahoma City, Oklahoma.

Yet, in 2008 they were back in New Orleans Arena, celebrating the franchise's first divisional championship. Under the direction of coach Byron Scott, the Hornets went on to win their first-round playoff series. They defeated the Dallas Mavericks four games to one. Point guard Chris Paul led the Hornets in scoring in Games 1 and 2. He scored 35 points in the opening game. West led the team in scoring in both Game 4 (24 points) and Game 5 (25 points).

Coach of the Year

In a stretch of just four years, former Los Angeles Laker Byron Scott led the Hornets from their worst season to their best. He also led them through Hurricane Katrina. The Hornets won just 18 games during his first season as coach, in 2004–05, but they blasted ahead to 56 wins and an NBA Southwest Division title in 2008. For that magical season, Scott was named the NBA's Coach of the Year. Previously, Scott had won three NBA championships as a player with the Lakers.

Just as they had done in the victory that had earned them the divisional championship, the Hornets clinched the playoff series win against Dallas in front of a sellout crowd at New Orleans Arena.

"A lot of people may be surprised with how this turned out, but we're not too surprised," West said.

The Hornets then won the first two games of their

"QUIET ASSASSIN"

A first-round pick in the 2005 NBA Draft, 6-foot-tall point guard Chris Paul quickly became a defensive star for the Hornets. He led the league in steals in three of his first four seasons, but he really shined in 2007–08. Paul ranked first in the NBA in both steals (217) and assists (925) that season. The 217 steals were a career high, and the 925 assists were a team record.

Paul made the NBA All-Star Game for the first time in 2008. He also led the Hornets in scoring with an average of 21.1 points per game, and he started 80 of the Hornets' 82 games. "CP3," his nickname, had become an NBA sensation. The "3" in his nickname comes from his jersey number. "He's a warrior," Hornets assistant coach Jim Cleamons said. "Don't be fooled by his demeanor and his little cherub smile. He's a quiet assassin."

second-round playoff series against the San Antonio Spurs. But the Spurs came back to win the series in seven games. That ended the Hornets' best season in team history. Scott was named the NBA's Coach of the Year.

Paul, who was playing in his third NBA season, averaged 21.1 points per game during the regular season. Paul became the first Hornet to be named to the All-NBA first team. Not even former Hornets stars Larry Johnson or Jamal Mashburn had that achievement. Paul's 56 double-doubles that season set a team record. Double-doubles are games in which a player records double figures of two different statistics, such as points and assists.

Paul and West both played in the 2008 NBA All-Star Game. West, a

Hornets forward David West, *right*, drives to the lane against Cleveland's Samardo Samuels in 2011. West was second on the team in scoring with 18.9 points per game.

first-round pick in the 2003 NBA Draft out of Xavier, averaged 20.6 points per game during the regular season. The Hornets had come a long way since their debut in Charlotte more than 20 years earlier.

Peja Power

On the night of November 6, 2007, in Los Angeles, Peja Stojakovic made Hornets history when he made 10 three-point shots in a 118–104 win over the Lakers. No other player had ever hit more than seven three-pointers against the Lakers. "The way he shot the ball tonight was unbelievable," said Hornets point guard Chris Paul, who had 21 assists in the game to set a team record.

CHAPTER 2

THE BUZZ ARRIVES

Charlotte, North Carolina, was known as the auto racing capital of the United States. And there were plenty of successful college basketball teams in the area. But there was no connection to a professional sports team of any kind in the state.

Many professional auto racers were based in cities located north and east of Charlotte. One of those towns was Kannapolis. It was the home of Dale Earnhardt. He won seven titles on the major auto racing circuit before he died in a crash in 2001. In nearby Concord, the Charlotte Motor Speedway was the area's only professional sports venue. Then George Shinn formed the Hornets for the 1988–89 NBA season.

Shinn was a Charlotte businessman who was born in Earnhardt's hometown of Kannapolis. He had earlier attempted to purchase a United States Football League Team,

Kelly Tripucka shows off the team's new road uniform in 1988. Tripucka led the team in scoring, averaging 22.6 points per game.

Businessman George Shinn, shown at a press conference in 1999, was the first owner of the Hornets.

Night of Firsts

On November 4, 1988, the Hornets played the Cleveland Cavaliers at the Charlotte Coliseum. It was the first game in club history. Forward Kelly Tripucka scored the team's first basket, and he also had the Hornets' first rebound and first steal. Even so, the Hornets lost the game 133–93. The starting lineup in the team's first game included Tripucka, forward Kurt Rambis, center Dave Hoppen, point guard Rickey Green, and shooting guard Robert Reid.

the Los Angeles Express. His plan had been to purchase the team and move it to Charlotte in 1984. After that failed, he launched a campaign in 1986 to obtain an NBA expansion team for Charlotte.

Despite having no arena and no team, Shinn's new ownership group had gotten the NBA's attention. They had

Hugo the Hornet

The Hornets' mascot, Hugo, has a piece of the Muppets in him. Cheryl Henson, daughter of Muppets creator Jim Henson, designed the mascot's outfit in 1988. The Muppets were puppet characters that had begun gaining fame in the 1970s. Hornets owner George Shinn had wanted Jim Henson involved, but Henson had requested too high a rate of pay for his work. He then suggested his daughter for the job. One of Cheryl Henson's friends wore the outfit, becoming the first mascot. "I just want it to be one mean bug," Shinn said in his book, You Gotta Believe!

managed to sell 8,400 season tickets within months after the campaign started—all in the hopes that a team would come to the city. And on April 1, 1987, after selling 12,000 season tickets, Shinn received the good news from NBA commissioner David Stern. Charlotte had been approved as the location for one of four NBA expansion teams. The new team would begin play in 1988. It would play in the brand new Charlotte Coliseum. The city of Charlotte had already begun constructing the arena in 1986.

Soon, "Hornets" was picked as the team's nickname. Its mascot was a giant bug known as Hugo. Famous clothing designer Alexander Julian designed the team's pinstripe uniforms. Dick Harter was the Hornets' first coach. And Rex Chapman of Kentucky was the team's first draft pick.

The Hornets' first win came on their third try. Former Notre Dame star forward Kelly Tripucka led the way with 24 points. Charlotte earned a 117–105 victory over the Los Angeles Clippers that night. Tripucka led the Hornets in scoring in their first season. He averaged 22.6 points per game. His teammate Kurt Rambis, a 6-foot-8 forward and former Los

The Muggsy Factor

One of the most popular Hornets in the team's early years was the NBA's shortest player, 5-foot-3 Tyrone "Muggsy" Bogues. Bogues had been known as Muggsy since his youth because of his ability to make defensive steals—to mug opponents. Bogues played for the Hornets for just over nine seasons. He ranked third in the NBA in assists with 867 during the 1989–90 season.

Angeles Laker, had 57 blocked shots that season. Rambis also led the team with 703 rebounds.

The Hornets won just 20 games in their first season. They had losing streaks that reached as many as nine games. They finished in last place in the Atlantic Division, 32 games behind the division champion New York Knicks. Still, the Hornets were a huge hit in Charlotte. After ending their season with a 120–110 loss on the road against the Boston Celtics, the city planned a celebration of the Hornets' first season. A parade through the streets of Charlotte drew thousands of fans.

It would take the Hornets five seasons and three head coaches to achieve a winning record. Even so, the Charlotte Coliseum was one of the toughest and noisiest home arenas in the NBA. The home court was known affectionately as "The Hive." Loud music played, and a loud Hornet-like buzz could be heard over the arena speakers. Spectators wore masks made to look like Rambis. And they even booed North Carolina hero Michael Jordan, a native of Wilmington, who was then playing for the Chicago Bulls.

The Hornets led the NBA in attendance during their first season. They even sold out their last 30 home games with crowds of 23,388. New York Knicks coach Rick Pitino said

Hornets guard Muggsy Bogues, *middle*, tries to guard Knicks center Patrick Ewing during a 1993 game. Bogues was only 5 feet 3 inches tall.

of The Hive, "I don't know if it's the music or what, but the noise in this place can just kill you."

In just a few short years, however, Hornets fans began singing a new tune.

Bench Star

The Hornets selected Dell Curry, one of their original players, in the 1988 expansion draft. Curry would go on to play 10 seasons for the Hornets, mostly as a guard coming off the bench. In 1993–94, when he averaged a career-high 16.3 points per game, Curry was named the NBA's Sixth Man of the Year.

CHAPTER 3

PLAYOFF MAGIC

NBA fever was riding high in Charlotte during the team's early years. Sellout crowds were regular at The Hive. But like many other expansion teams, losses were plentiful. In their first three seasons, the Hornets did not win more than 26 games in an 82-game schedule. Then, one day in 1991, luck changed everything.

The Hornets won the NBA Draft lottery. The lottery is a system used by the NBA to determine the order in which teams select players entering the league. With the first number one pick in team history, the Hornets selected University of Nevada, Las Vegas (UNLV) star Larry Johnson. They signed the 6-foot-6 forward to a contract that included $1.9 million in his first season.

Johnson averaged 19.2 points and 11 rebounds per game during his rookie season

Hornets forward Larry Johnson, *center*, drives past Boston Celtics players during a 1995 game. Johnson was the NBA Rookie of the Year in 1992.

Hot Streak

Larry Johnson recorded the first triple-double in Hornets history on March 18, 1993. A triple-double occurs when a player reaches double-digit totals in any three of the following five statistical categories: points, rebounds, assists, steals, and blocked shots. That night, Johnson scored 11 points and had a team-high 12 rebounds and 10 assists in a 113–85 win over the Minnesota Timberwolves in Charlotte. He then followed his achievement with another triple-double the next night in Indiana. He totaled 21 points, 11 assists, and 10 rebounds in a 112–108 loss to the Indiana Pacers.

in 1991–92. He was named the NBA's Rookie of the Year. And he had a club-record 23 rebounds in a game against the Minnesota Timberwolves.

Johnson quickly emerged as a team leader for the Hornets. His outgoing personality was a big hit. He would eventually star as "Grandmama" in a series of television commercials for a brand of basketball shoes. In the commercials, he put on a dress, wore glasses, and performed a variety of slam dunks and tricky basketball moves.

On the court, the Hornets won a team-best 31 games in Johnson's rookie season. The following season, in 1992–93, they won 44 games. That was good enough to get the team into the playoffs for the first time. The Hornets even won a series, beating the Boston Celtics three games to one. However, the New York Knicks eliminated the Hornets in the second round.

Johnson set a team record for baskets (728) in a season. He was also a starter for the Eastern Conference team in the NBA All-Star Game.

In addition to Johnson, the Hornets were bolstered by 6-foot-10 center Alonzo Mourning. The Hornets had

Charlotte center Alonzo Mourning, *back left*, holds the ball over two Knicks players in a 1993 playoff game.

Rookie Blocker

Former Georgetown star Alonzo Mourning quickly made his presence known as a rookie with the Hornets in 1992–93. The second pick in the 1992 NBA Draft, Mourning started in 78 games and was named to the NBA All-Rookie team. Mourning's 271 blocked shots ranked fourth in the NBA that season and set a club record that still stood through the 2010–11 season.

selected the former Georgetown star with the second pick in the 1992 NBA Draft. Johnson and Mourning combined for an average of 43.1 points and 20.8 rebounds per game during the 1992–93 season. Their efforts helped lead the Hornets to the postseason for the first time.

Although the Hornets lost to the Knicks four games to one, Charlotte had carved a path to NBA success. The Hornets made the playoffs in three of the next five seasons. They even won 50 games for the first time in 1994–95. However, they would not win another playoff series until 1998.

In the 1996–97 season, first-year coach David Cowens replaced former head coach Allan Bristow. The Hornets won 54 games that season. That was a team record for wins. And this time, there was no Grandmama or Mourning. Johnson, whose salary had grown to $4.2 million in 1995–96, was traded to the Knicks in July 1996. Similarly, Mourning was dealt to the Miami Heat in a huge seven-player trade in November 1995.

Hello, Boston

After posting their first winning record in 1992–93, the Hornets were rewarded with a first-round playoff series against the Boston Celtics. The Boston Garden had been the home of legendary NBA players such as Larry Bird, Bob Cousy, John Havlicek, and coach Red Auerbach. The Celtics won Game 1 in the Hornets' playoff debut on April 29, 1993. But Charlotte answered with three consecutive wins to capture the series. Alonzo Mourning sent the Celtics home for the summer with a buzzer-beating, 20-foot jump shot for a 104–103 win in Game 4.

Despite losing two of their stars, the Hornets plowed to fourth place in the Central Division and another playoff appearance that season. That was thanks in large part to Glen Rice. He was one of the players who arrived in the Mourning deal. He averaged a career-best 26.8 points per game, which

Hornets forward Glen Rice goes for a dunk during the 1997 All-Star Game. Rice was named the MVP of the game.

Hornets guard Bobby Phills battles Wally Szczerbiak of the Minnesota Timberwolves for a loose ball in 1999. Phills died in a car accident on January 12, 2000.

ranked third in the league. He also scored a club-record 48 points in a 122–121 overtime victory against the Boston Celtics in March 1997.

Beginning with the 1996–97 season, the Hornets entered an impressive seven-year stretch. During that time, they had a winning record every season. They even reached the Eastern Conference semifinals three times.

But there were also bad days. In October 1999, Hornets guard Eldridge Recasner suffered a partially collapsed lung in a car accident. He was a passenger in a car driven by teammate Derrick Coleman. Then, in January 2000, veteran Hornets guard Bobby Phills was killed in a car accident after a team practice. He died while racing teammate David Wesley. Team owner George Shinn called it "the ultimate tragedy."

Beginning with the 1999–2000 season, the Hornets began a stretch in which they qualified for the playoffs in five consecutive years. But The Hive was buzzing with trouble. Shinn wanted a new arena. However, Charlotte city officials did not believe the Hornets needed one. Shinn then threatened to move the team. That led to the loss of some of the Hornets' fans.

By the 2001–02 season, Shinn had closed a deal with the NBA to move the team to New Orleans. The Louisiana city had been home to the Jazz during the 1970s. It was known

Remembering Bobby

Ten years after a high-speed car crash killed former Hornets player Bobby Phills, his wife continued to speak about the tragedy at Charlotte-area schools. And she still maintained possession of the crumpled Porsche car that Phills was driving at the time of his death. "Bobby's death was a horrible thing, but a lot of wonderful things have come out of it. The support we have received in Charlotte has been overwhelming, and that's why we never left," Kendall Phills said.

for hosting major sporting events such as the Super Bowl. Shinn hoped the team would have more success there. In Charlotte, the Hornets' home attendance had dropped to an average of 11,286. That was not even half of the Charlotte Coliseum's total capacity.

CHAPTER 4

OFF TO
NEW ORLEANS

W hen the Hornets arrived in New Orleans, they were greeted by cheering fans and a sellout crowd of 17,668. Everyone was there to see the Hornets in their 2002–03 season opener against the Utah Jazz.

The Jazz had played in New Orleans as an NBA expansion team from 1974 to 1979, before moving to Utah. It had been more than 20 years since New Orleans had another NBA team to call its own.

The Hornets won that first game 100–75, behind 21 points from point guard Baron Davis. New Orleans then won their next 10 home games to break the franchise record for consecutive home wins.

The Jazz had played in the massive Louisiana Superdome during much of their time in New Orleans. The Hornets played in the more traditionally sized New Orleans Arena. The Jazz also had a superstar during their time in New Orleans.

Hornets guard Baron Davis drives past Zydrunas Ilgauskas of the Cleveland Cavaliers in 2004.

Hornets forward Jamal Mashburn drives past Morris Peterson of the Toronto Raptors in 2003. Mashburn averaged more than 20 points a game during his four seasons with the team.

Home, "Suite" Home

The New Orleans Arena is no Louisiana Superdome, but it does sit right next to it. When owner George Shinn moved the Hornets to New Orleans, the new arena attracted him to the city. The arena had 56 executive suites, 2,800 club seats, and a parking lot that it shared with the Superdome. The Arena was built in 1999. It is also home to the Tulane University basketball teams.

"Pistol Pete" Maravich was a basketball legend both in college at Louisiana State and with the Jazz. The Hornets retired his No. 7 jersey at halftime of the season-opening game.

Instead of one superstar, the Hornets had many good players. Among them was Jamal Mashburn. He was a former first-round draft pick of the Dallas Mavericks. Mashburn had averaged more than 20 points per game the previous two seasons. In addition, Davis, the third pick in the 1999 draft, had ranked fourth in the league in assists in 2001–02. He made the NBA All-Star Game that season. And former Kentucky star Jamaal Magloire, a 6-foot-11 center, stepped in when veteran Elden Campbell underwent knee surgery.

The Hornets won 15 of their first 21 games. They did not lose at home until the Los Angeles Clippers stole a four-point win in the second week of December. Then, an eight-game winning streak in February and March was followed by a five-game winning streak to end the season. That left the Hornets with a 47–35 record. They placed third in the Central Division and faced the

Monster Mash

They call him "Monster Mash." Jamal Mashburn came to the Hornets in 2000 as part of a nine-player deal with the Miami Heat. By the time the Hornets moved to New Orleans in 2002, Mashburn's annual salary was up to $7.75 million. He lived up to the money. Mashburn averaged a team-leading 21.6 points per game in 2002–03, his highest scoring average in seven seasons. He also was named to the 2003 NBA All-Star Game. On February 21, 2003, Mashburn set the Hornets' single-game scoring record when he scored 50 points in an overtime win against the Memphis Grizzlies.

Philadelphia 76ers in a first-round playoff series.

The 76ers defeated the Hornets four games to two. However, the season still produced some highlights for the Hornets. Mashburn scored a club-record 50 points in an overtime win against the Memphis Grizzlies. He was named an NBA All-Star for the first time. And he averaged a 21.6 points per game that season. That was his highest scoring average as a member of the Hornets.

Davis broke out with a successful season in 2003–04. He averaged a career-high 22.9 points and 2.4 steals per game. He was named an NBA All-Star for the second time.

That same season, Magloire started all 82 games. He averaged 13.6 points and 10.3 rebounds per game. Both were career highs. In 2004, Magloire and Davis became the first Hornets duo named to the NBA All-Star team since Larry Johnson and Alonzo Mourning in 1995. They led the Hornets to a 17–7 start to the regular season. But the team finished just 41–41 and placed third in the Central Division. That marked the Hornets' first non-winning campaign in eight seasons.

From there, the Hornets clearly became a rebuilding

Dynamic Duo

Guard Baron Davis, the third pick in the 1999 NBA Draft, and center Jamaal Magloire, the 19th pick in the 2000 Draft, were important parts of the Hornets in 2003–04 and beyond. In 2004, they were the first Hornets duo to be named to the NBA All-Star Game since Larry Johnson and Alonzo Mourning in 1995. Magloire had 45 double-doubles in 2003–04. And that same season, Davis ranked second in the NBA in steals (158) and three-pointers (187), seventh in assists (501), and sixth in points per game (22.9).

project. Tim Floyd lasted as coach for just one season, 2003–04. Former Lakers star Byron Scott then took over. Scott started his tenure with an 18-win season in 2004–05. And during that year, the team made even more personnel moves. David Wesley, an eight-year Hornet, was traded to the Houston Rockets in December. Davis, in his sixth season with the Hornets, was traded to the

Hornets center Jamaal Magloire grabs a rebound against the Denver Nuggets in 2005. He was an NBA All-Star in 2004.

Golden State Warriors in February. And Mashburn was sent to the Philadelphia 76ers the same day Davis was traded.

The Hornets began that season with an eight-game losing streak. They then defeated the Jazz, but they lost another 11 straight after that. Their scoring average of 88.4 points per game ranked last in the league. They also ranked last in the league in attendance.

But the biggest storm to hit New Orleans had not yet arrived. That would come in August 2005.

CHAPTER 5

THE HURRICANE YEARS

The Hornets were less than five weeks away from starting training camp in 2005 when the storm hit New Orleans.

Hurricane Katrina made landfall on August 29, 2005. It pounded the Louisiana coast as a Category 3 storm. Winds reached 125 mph (201 kph). In its wake, the storm left behind severe flooding. Approximately 250,000 residents had to leave their homes because 80 percent of New Orleans was flooded.

The storm did an estimated $125 billion in damage.

For days, the Hornets could not even locate all of their players and staff members. Many of them had left the city. Suddenly, the Hornets were faced not with winning games, but with survival. The rest of the city was, too.

Floodwaters from Hurricane Katrina fill the streets near downtown New Orleans on August 30, 2005.

"Because we were displaced like everybody else, it really created a bond between us and people in this area," said Hornets equipment manager David Jovanovic. He had to have his home completely rebuilt as a result of the destruction.

Less than a month after the hurricane hit, the Hornets announced they would move all operations to Oklahoma City, Oklahoma. Upon advice from the NBA, the Hornets would play the majority of their games the next two seasons at Ford Center in Oklahoma City. The team and the league decided upon Oklahoma City because it had previously expressed interest in joining the NBA.

New Orleans Arena itself had not been hit hard, but the flooding around the arena and power failures made the prospect of playing an NBA game there impossible.

Although New Orleans Arena was eventually capable of holding games, the city could not support an NBA team at the time. Still, the team played three games in New Orleans in March 2006 and six more in 2006–07. They also played a few games at other locations in Louisiana and Oklahoma.

On November 1, 2005, the Hornets made their Oklahoma City debut. They defeated the Sacramento Kings 93–67 in front of a capacity crowd at the Ford Center. The evening began with a street party outside the arena. It featured bands, face painting, and other activities to celebrate the city's new, temporarily placed team.

Hornets guard J. R. Smith shoots a layup in 2005. In his first season with the Hornets, Smith averaged 10.3 points per game.

Hornets guard Chris Paul, *left*, scores two of his 25 points against the Atlanta Hawks in 2005.

"It's a great city, full of great fans," said guard J. R. Smith, who scored 19 points in the opening-night victory.

The New Orleans Hornets became the New Orleans/ Oklahoma City Hornets. They wore an "OKC" patch on their uniforms to recognize their temporary home. They also welcomed a new player. Rookie point guard Chris Paul led the NBA with 175 steals and ranked fifth in the league with 611 assists in 2005–06. He had been a star at Wake Forest in college. And he was the fourth pick in the 2005 NBA Draft. He became the second Hornets player to be named the NBA's

Rookie Sensation

Chris Paul's impact as the Hornets' point guard in 2005 was immediate. In fact, some wondered later how he had fallen all the way to the fourth pick in the 2005 NBA Draft. Paul finished his first season as the NBA steals leader. He was only the second rookie in league history to achieve that honor. And he had 124 of 125 first-place votes to be named the NBA's Rookie of the Year.

Rookie of the Year, after Larry Johnson. Paul dominated the league's other rookies. He ranked first among rookies in points, assists, steals, minutes played, double-doubles, and triple-doubles.

Paul and forward David West led the Hornets to a dramatic improvement from the previous season. West had been a first-round pick in the 2003 NBA Draft. He averaged 17.1 points per game in 2005–06. Paul averaged 16.1 points per game. The Hornets went from 18 wins in 2004–05 to 38 wins in 2005–06. They finished in fourth place in the Southwest Division and missed the playoffs by just six wins.

In 2006–07, the Hornets increased their win total to 39. They played all but six of their home games in Oklahoma City, as hurricane reconstruction was still taking place. Paul raised his scoring average to 17.3 points per game and ranked fourth in the NBA with 8.9 assists per game that season.

The Hornets were drawing so well in Oklahoma City that there was even talk of moving the club there permanently. Instead, the Hornets returned to New Orleans in 2007. Oklahoma City then got its own team in 2008. The former Seattle SuperSonics team moved there, becoming the Oklahoma City Thunder.

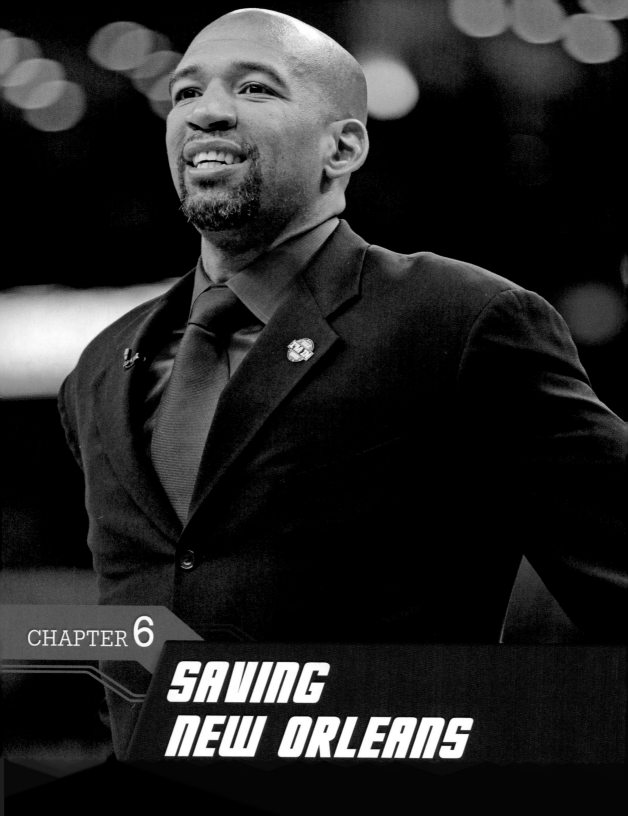

CHAPTER **6**

SAVING
NEW ORLEANS

The Hornets returned home in 2007–08 and promptly won their first division championship in New Orleans. Chris Paul and forward David West again led the team. In the playoffs, the Hornets dispatched the Dallas Mavericks in the first round. Then they took the San Antonio Spurs to a deciding seventh game in the second round.

Paul continued his domination from the point guard position in 2008–09. He made his second consecutive NBA All-Star Game appearance. He again led the league in steals and assists. And his 22.8 points-per-game average was the highest of his first six pro seasons. West added a career-high 21 points per game. West was also in the NBA All-Star Game for the second straight year.

However, the Hornets' lineup dropped in production

Monty Williams took over as coach of the Hornets before the start of the 2010–11 season and led them into the playoffs with a 46–36 record.

HELPING RECOVER

The Hornets played a leading role in trying to help save the city of New Orleans after Hurricane Katrina hit in 2005. In 2008, New Orleans hosted the NBA All-Star Game. All-Star players and former NBA stars worked alongside thousands of volunteers to improve the city. They teamed up to rebuild homes, schools, and playgrounds at 10 different locations across New Orleans.

Hornets' team owner George Shinn funded the Hoops for Homes project. His Shinn Foundation allowed for 65 homes to be repaired and rebuilt. A number of service organizations also partnered with the Hornets. That allowed the Hoops for Homes program to be extended to teachers, and offered $1.2 million in grants and home repair funding to New Orleans–based schoolteachers.

after Paul and West. Sharpshooting guard Peja Stojakovic's 13.3 points per game average was his lowest in nine seasons. And the Hornets ranked just 26th in the NBA in rebounds. Tyson Chandler led the team with 8.7 rebounds per game, but he only played in 45 games due to an ankle injury.

The Hornets won 49 games in 2008–09. That tied for the fifth-best win total in club history. But the team fell to fourth place in the Southwest Division. They lost six of their final eight regular-season games. They then quickly lost in five games to the Denver Nuggets in the first round of the playoffs.

Despite their overall success, attendance at home games in New Orleans was low. The Hornets averaged just more than 14,000 fans per

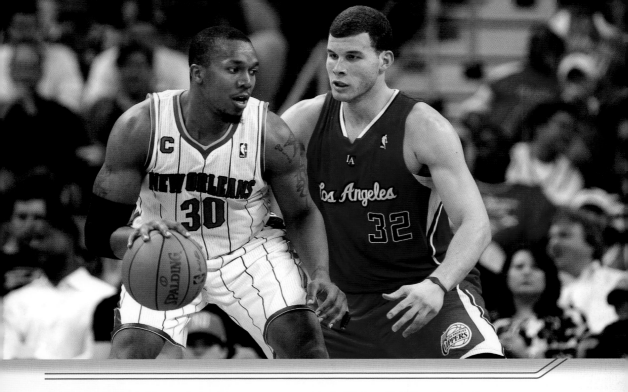

Forward David West, *left*, tries to get around Blake Griffin of the Los Angeles Clippers during a 2011 game.

game in 2007–08. They jumped to just under 17,000 fans per game during the next season. The team had attracted more fans in their two seasons in Oklahoma City.

The Hornets' home attendance fell to around 15,000 fans per game in 2009–10. That season, the Hornets team record also fell to 37–45. Coach Byron Scott was fired after a 3–6 start.

First Picks

The Hornets traded away their top choices in the 2008 and 2010 NBA Drafts. They were 2010 first-rounder Cole Aldrich of Kansas and 2008 first-rounder Darrell Arthur of Kansas. Arthur went to the Portland Trail Blazers for cash. And Aldrich, along with Morris Peterson, was dealt to the Oklahoma City Thunder for the rights to first-round picks Craig Brackins and Quincy Pondexter. Brackins was then sent to the Philadelphia 76ers before the 2010–11 season began.

Los Angeles Lakers guard Kobe Bryant, *left*, goes up for a shot as Hornets center Emeka Okafor, *right*, defends during the 2011 playoffs.

West averaged 19 points per game in 2009–10. But Paul

Fresh Face

"Monty is one of the players that I played with and coached. It makes you feel 1,000 years old."
—Doc Rivers, who coached Monty Williams in Orlando and played with him in 1994–95 in New York. Williams was a 1994 first-round pick out of Notre Dame by the Knicks.

played just 45 games due to a knee injury that required surgery. The Hornets finished 37–45 and dropped to last place in the Southwest Division. They missed the playoffs for the first time in three years.

The Hornets hired Monty Williams as coach for the 2010–11 season. His efforts were immediately boosted by Paul's presence. The point guard started all but two games for the Hornets. And, for the third time in his career, he led the NBA in steals per game at 2.4.

West led the Hornets with 18.9 points per game. Center Emeka Okafor, gave him support under the hoop. They combined for 17.1 rebounds per game. Behind those three players, the Hornets finished 46–36 and returned to the playoffs. However, West missed the playoffs with a knee injury. Without him, the Hornets lost to the two-time defending champion Los Angeles Lakers in the first round.

Despite the Hornets' above-average play on the court, they struggled to attract fans. Only four teams had fewer fans in 2010–11. Shinn tried to sell the team, but could not find a buyer. In December 2010, the NBA took over the team.

In Charge

At age 38, Monty Williams became the NBA's youngest head coach when he took over the Hornets in June 2010. It was his first head coaching job after interning as a coach for the San Antonio Spurs in 2004–05 and joining the Portland Trail Blazers as an assistant coach in 2005–06. "We don't view it as a gamble. We view it as an opportunity," Hornets general manager Jeff Bower said at the time. The Hornets won their first eight games on their way to the playoffs in 2010–11.

League officials expressed interest in keeping the team in New Orleans. They were seeking local ownership to keep the team there.

With a young coach—Williams, who was 38 when he was hired in 2010, was the youngest NBA head coach—and a strong core of players behind Paul, West, and Okafor, the Hornets appear to have a bright future. Fans are just hoping that future is in New Orleans.

TIMELINE

1987
Charlotte, North Carolina, is one of four expansion franchises approved by the NBA on April 22. The Hornets and the Miami Heat would begin play at the start of the 1988–89 season.

1988
The Hornets play their first game in franchise history on November 4. They lose to the Cleveland Cavaliers 133–93 in front of a near-sellout crowd of 23,338 at the Charlotte Coliseum.

1991
Holding the first number one NBA Draft pick in club history, the Hornets select NCAA Player of the Year Larry Johnson of the University of Nevada, Las Vegas on June 26. Johnson would play for the Hornets the next five seasons, making the NBA All-Star Game twice.

1993
Johnson scores the first triple-double in club history on March 18 behind 11 points, 12 rebounds, and 10 assists in a 113–85 win over Minnesota.

1993
The Hornets play the first playoff game in club history on April 29, losing 112–101 to the Boston Celtics. The Hornets would go on to defeat the Celtics in the next three games to win the series, three games to one.

2000
Hornets player Bobby Phills is killed in a car crash on January 12 following practice, when he was drag-racing with teammate David Wesley. Later, Wesley is found guilty of reckless driving, is fined $250, and is sentenced to 40 hours of community service.

2002
On May 10, the NBA approved Hornets owner George Shinn's request to move the team from Charlotte to New Orleans.

2002	On October 30, the New Orleans Hornets play the Utah Jazz, formerly the New Orleans Jazz, in their first game at their new home, the New Orleans Arena. The Hornets defeat the Jazz 100–75, beginning a franchise-record 11–0 home-court winning streak.
2005	Forced out of New Orleans by Hurricane Katrina, the New Orleans/Oklahoma City Hornets begin their season on November 1 with a 93–67 win over Sacramento at the Ford Center in Oklahoma City, Oklahoma. The Hornets would play in four different home arenas in 2005–06.
2007	Point guard Chris Paul assists on 21 baskets in a 118–104 victory over the Los Angeles Lakers on November 6. It is a club record. On the same night, Peja Stojakovic hits a club-record 10 three-point baskets.
2008	Back in the refurbished New Orleans Arena, the Hornets capture the first divisional championship in club history with a 114–92 win over the Los Angeles Clippers on April 15. The victory clinches first place in the Southwest Division.
2010	On June 8, Monty Williams is named head coach of the Hornets. He is the ninth head coach in the club's history and the youngest in the NBA at age 38.
2010	On December 6, NBA commissioner David Stern says that the league will take over ownership of the Hornets due to financial struggles by owner George Shinn.
2011	The Hornets return to the playoffs, with David West averaging 18.9 points per game during the regular season to lead the team. They are eliminated in the first round.

QUICK STATS

FRANCHISE HISTORY

Charlotte Hornets (1988–2002)
New Orleans Hornets (2002–05,
2007–)
New Orleans/Oklahoma City
Hornets (2005–07)

NBA FINALS

None

DIVISION CHAMPIONSHIPS

2008

PLAYOFF APPEARANCES

1993, 1995, 1997, 1998, 2000, 2001,
2002, 2003, 2004, 2008, 2009, 2011

KEY PLAYERS
(position[s]; years with team)

Tyrone "Muggsy" Bogues (G;
   1988–97)
Rex Chapman (G; 1988–92)
Dell Curry (G/F; 1988–98)
Baron Davis (G; 1999–05)
Larry Johnson (F; 1991–96)
Jamal Mashburn (F; 2000–04)
Alonzo Mourning (C; 1992–95)
Chris Paul (G; 2005–)
J. R. Reid (F/C; 1989–92, 1997–99)
Glen Rice (F; 1995–98)
Peja Stojakovic (F/G; 2006–10)
Kelly Tripucka (F; 1988–91)
David West (F; 2003–)

KEY COACHES

Allan Bristow (1991–96):
   207–203; 5–8 (postseason)
Byron Scott (2004–09):
   203–216; 8–9 (postseason)

HOME ARENAS

Charlotte Coliseum (1988–02)
Lloyd Noble Center (2005–06)
Ford Center (2005–06, 2006–07)
New Orleans Arena (2002–05,
   2007–)

* All statistics through 2010–11 season

QUOTES AND ANECDOTES

The first sellout in Hornets history came on November 26, 1988, in Charlotte against the Washington Bullets. More than 23,000 fans were at the Charlotte Coliseum. The Bullets won the game, but coach Wes Unseld was hoping for some divine help during a timeout in the midst of all that noise. "I told the guys, 'Men, bow your heads and pray they shut up. It's our only chance.'"

George Shinn, the Hornets' first owner, tried to obtain Larry Brown as the team's first head coach in the same year that Brown won the NCAA men's basketball championship at Kansas. When Shinn could not get Brown, he opted for Dick Harter, whose appearance by itself impressed Shinn more than the other candidates. "Dick was the only one with a suit and a white shirt. He looked good. I like that."

New Orleans basketball is known for more than the Hornets, "Pistol Pete" Maravich, and games at the Louisiana Superdome. In 1977, the New Orleans Jazz (now Utah) made NBA history when they drafted Lusia Harris of Delta State in the seventh round of the NBA Draft. She was the first woman to be drafted by an NBA team.

Although the Hornets and the Tulane University basketball teams became the main tenants at New Orleans Arena, the first event at the $84 million arena was a New Orleans Brass minor league hockey game in October 1999.

"All my life, people have been telling me I'm too small to compete on the next level. But basketball isn't for big people; it's for people who can play the game."
—Tyrone "Muggsy" Bogues, discussing how he has overcome his lack of height

GLOSSARY

assist

A pass that leads directly to a made basket.

attendance

The number of fans at a particular game or who come to watch a team play during a particular season.

contract

A binding agreement about, for example, years of commitment by a basketball player in exchange for a given salary.

debut

A first appearance.

draft

A system used by professional sports leagues to select new players in order to spread incoming talent among all teams. The NBA Draft is held each June.

expansion

In sports, the addition of a franchise or franchises to a league.

franchise

An entire sports organization, including the players, coaches, and staff.

general manager

The executive who is in charge of the team's overall operation. He or she hires and fires coaches, drafts players, and signs free agents.

overtime

A period in a basketball game that is played to determine a winner when the four quarters end in a tie.

rebound

To secure the basketball after a missed shot.

retire

To officially end one's career.

rookie

A first-year player in the NBA.

trade

A move in which a player or players are sent from one team to another.

FOR MORE INFORMATION

Further Reading

Ballard, Chris. *The Art of a Beautiful Game: The Thinking Fan's Tour of the NBA.* New York: Simon & Schuster, 2009.

Shinn, George. *You Gotta Believe!* Carol Stream, Ill.: Tyndale House Publishers, 1996.

Simmons, Bill. *The Book of Basketball: The NBA According to the Sports Guy.* New York: Random House, 2009.

Web Links

To learn more about the New Orleans Hornets, visit ABDO Publishing Company online at **www.abdopublishing.com**. Web sites about the Hornets are featured on our Book Links page. These links are routinely monitored and updated to provide the most current information available.

Places to Visit

Louisiana Sports Hall of Fame
500 Front Street
Natchitoches, LA 71457
318-238-4255
www.lasportshall.com
The Louisiana Sports Hall of Fame Museum includes exhibits profiling Hall of Fame inductees, professional teams, and college teams.

Naismith Memorial Basketball Hall of Fame
1000 W. Columbus, Ave.
Springfield, MA 01105
413-781-6500
www.hoophall.com
This hall of fame and museum highlights the greatest players and moments in the history of basketball. Robert Parish, who played for the Hornets from 1994 to 1996, is enshrined here.

New Orleans Arena
1501 Girod Street
New Orleans, LA 70113
504-587-3808
www.neworleansarena.com
This has been the Hornets' home arena since 2002, when they moved to New Orleans from Charlotte. The team plays 41 regular-season games here each year.

INDEX

About the Author

Paul D. Bowker is a freelance writer and author based in Ponte Vedra, Florida. He is also a former sports editor who wrote about the Hornets during their early seasons in Charlotte. Bowker has covered several NBA Finals during a 25-year newspaper career, and he has won multiple national, regional, and state writing awards. He is a past president of Associated Press Sports Editors, as well. Bowker lives with his wife and daughter.